STOCKHOLM SYNDROME

CAN WE CALL IT LOVE?

K. DISHA

ISBN 979-888530553-2

This book is dedicated to my family who always supported me and made me capable for writing this book. I am thankful to them for never leaving my side.

Contents

PREFACE

I, as a student as well as a writer was always interested in human psychology and behavior. Stockholm syndrome is a concept which always diverted my interest and forced me to write this book. Stockholm syndrome is a psychological connection which occurs when hostages develop some bond with their captors, and as such many consider it to be a psychological condition but i was always curious about one thing, can Stockholm syndrome be called a real love? And with that curiosity I wrote this book.

Acknowledgements

Writing this book was very special for me. While writing it my family supported me immensely especially my brother whose criticisms helped me a lot in improving my writing.

PROLOGUE

The Book revolves around the story of Sara, a young graduate who dreams of working and earning generously., As a young woman with an optimistic and extrovert personality, Sara was persuading her Master's degree and decides to leave her home town to get a better job and gain freedom but suddenly one day her life turns upside down when she meets Karan.

What will happen to Sara after her brief encounter with Karan? Will she be able to achieve what she aims for, or will Karan break all her dreams? Can Sara still grow like a butterfly with warm and beautiful colors?

I

LASS FULL OF DREAMS, HAPPINESS AND GOALS

My life was beautiful. Maybe, But I think it ultimately depends on a person about how he/she perceives their life. I was always an extrovert, surrounded by many friends and people around me, I was living my life like a social butterfly, a butterfly which is always happy and was never serious about anything in life. I never felt any need to worry about anything except for my father. My father was an extreme believer of justice, orthodox at the same time and on top of that he was an extremely disciplined person. I was free outside but there was a limitation to my freedom as well. My father was a retired police man, mother always respects my father and never opposes his decisions and it's not because of fear or suppression but maybe because she trusted him blindly. She was not the type of a lady depended on her husband for everything but rather she was a very strong independent woman who worked as a company manager.

I always wanted to be like my mother but sometimes I experienced that she was somewhat trapped and not living her life to the fullest. But I was not like my mother! I had my own dreams to achieve and live a happy life free from all the family bonds and restrictions.

"You will be graduated next month and it's good for you to get married and settle down" my father concluded

'What? But father... I don't want to marry so early, i want to get my Master's degree and then work on a decent job for my whole life!' I exclaimed

"I am not stopping you from studying further; it's just that I care for you..."

'What kind of care is this father? You are just obstructing my dreams'

"I took this decision in consideration of your well being. I just want you to get married and then continue your studies and work, what's wrong in that?"

'Father, everything is wrong! I just don't want to get married!'

"But what is wrong in getting married? Perhaps... do you have any boyfriend out there?"

'No! I don't have any boyfriend. Father, do you think I could top in my college while hanging around with a man?'

(Sigh) "If not then what is the problem with you?"

'I... I just don't want to get married that's it!'

My mother observed my sullen expression and she also got the hint that my father was getting frustrated she couldn't just let us argue anymore and stepped in as a mediator,

"Stop it both of you! Do you think this is your debate competition Sara? Where are your manners?" my mother started scolding me

'But mom... father started it!'

"Apologize to your father right now!"

'Sorry father...' I felt extremely sad. It wasn't even my fault! I didn't even start any conversation but why am I being scolded and for what I am apologizing for?

"And you... (Sigh) why are you forcing her to marry? What's the matter?" she asked my father worriedly

"I went for a morning walk and there I stumbled upon a rock and was about to fall when a young man gripped my hand and helped me, he looked familiar to me but i didn't know who he was..."

"And... don't tell me you concluded to marry your daughter to any random man whom you met on streets"

"Let me just complete first!"

"Fine then continue..."

"Ahem! So that young man helped me and looked very familiar to me and as I was wondering, 'where I saw him?' his father came to me asked whether I was okay and at that time you won't believe whom I met!"

'Whom did you meet?'

"My superior from our police department! He was one of the most reputed and best officers I have ever met in my whole life! And his son was very promising young man. I had a walk with them and also spend my time and got to know that he is searching for a girl to marry his son, at that moment I thought why not Sara and him..."

'Father no!'

"Why? Sara you can't perceive your career in this small town and you have to go to some other place to complete your studies as well as to work in a reputed company and I don't feel comfortable in sending you away from us... (Sigh) you were always in our care and protection, with your personality you always shine very brightly and as a result many people will have eyes on you, I was a police officer and my experience teaches me not to be ignorant of any possible threats"

'But father I am not the only girl who is going outside the town to study, there are many other girls who stay in hostel and it is safe out there... I can understand your fear father, since you were always surrounded by criminals and crime that you have suspicion on every little thing but if you keep hiding me like that then how can I learn?'

I tried to convince my father as much as possible. I knew he was worried for me but that doesn't mean that I am going to marry any random man of my father's choice! My main goal is to stay single and enjoy my life to the fullest. I don't want to get entangled in any relationship and keep getting stressed.

My mother was calmly listening, she didn't rely and neither reacted she just stood with an expressionless face which makes any person hard to depict what was going on in her mind and then after a long pause she spoke,

" I think Sara is right..." with just those words I sighed with relief, since I knew that if my mother supported father then it was impossible for me to convince both and had to accept their decision.

"But that doesn't mean I completely disagree with what your father is saying..." these words left me speechless. So does that mean she is agreeing with my father?

"Sara I think you should concentrate on studies for now and complete your Master's, then when you get job we will think about your engagement"

Though her words was a bit unconvincing to me but as long as the problem is solved I can sigh with relief, for now I should just concentrate on my studies and when I get job and start earning I will leave this house and start living on my own, I was thinking of just leaving my house with those thoughts in my mind.

I was really naive and was always careless in my behavior, I studied hard just to show my good results to my parents so that they don't nag me but now… now things were really different. There was a dream to achieve something and get away from all the restrictions, there was hope to find happiness and there was aim to my aimless life, I started feeling a sense of responsibility, perhaps this is what we call growing up? I just don't know but I was full of determination this time… I was so determined that I didn't hear my parents conversation and just nodded

"Okay then it's decided you will stay in Pomona Auntie's house for completing your studies" my mother smiled

'W-What? Who is Pomona auntie?'

"Oh she is my brother's wife's best friend; we met in my brother's wedding… Don't you remember?"

Me and my father stared at each other and gave an awkward smile, we both knew how obsessed mother was with her family and relationships, indeed her connections were great.

'Mom I don't want to stay in some unknown person's house'

"What do you mean by unknown person? I know her very well"

'But I don't know her and rather than staying in the house of some random people I think hostel is more comfortable for me'

I decided to leave because now I knew that if I stayed any longer then my parents will surely bring up some or the other topic and it was really problematic so I just left and went to my friend Meera's house. Meera was my childhood friend and we both stayed together almost every time, my mother hates Meera, I just don't know the proper reason but she just doesn't like her but that doesn't mean I can just give up on my friendship with her.

I met Meera when I was in kindergarten, we were very young back then but Meera was always shy and reserve and nobody approached her neither communicated with her even teachers there maintained an awkward relationship with her. I as the first to approach her and we became friends very quickly. She was not bright and not beautiful either and because of that she always was depressed and had some sort of inferiority complex and she still has it till now. As time passed by I slowly understood why people stayed away from her. It was because she was the daughter of a mistress and was forcibly acknowledged as daughter by her father, her father didn't possess much affection for her and ignored her most of the time. My mother was reluctant to accept her as my friend, she even expressed her displeasure sometimes but I just like Meera the way she is...

'Hey? Were you waiting for me?' I smiled brightly when I saw her

"Oh no... Not at all" she smiled slyly and while tucking her hair back she asked me "So you are coming with me right? I know I am asking more from you but you know I just can't stay alone in that big and unknown place without anyone's help..."

'Oh come on! I will always be with you so don't worry!' I assured her and then we started planning on what all things we will do when we leave our home town and go there.

Things won't go as planned most of the time and a similar situation occurred with me and Meera, Meera's father who was never interested in her asked her to stay for few more days as there was some emergency and thus Meera stayed here and as planned I went to continue my studies, Meera promised me that she will come to me as soon as her work ends, I agreed and explored the city to get adapted. My sense of direction was very poor and thus I studied each and every detail I observed and prepared a map out of it. My map was ready and so was I. I was still exploring the city and didn't visit my hostel. After completing all the procedures and submitting numerous documents they allowed me to enter the Hostel but before entering I was introduced with a long list of rules to be followed and most of them were boring but still after agreeing with them I was finally into my hostel room.

II
FREEDOM

'Freedom' how important is this word in each and everyone's life… for me freedom just meant getting away from all the naggings and scolding's from my parents it was all about escaping and living freely with no worries and thus I, for the very first time felt a sense of freedom when I entered my hostel room. I was away from my parents all alone without any friends, without any support and this was all happening for the very first time in my life. As an only child to my parents, all their attention, all their care, love was directed towards me effortlessly. I enjoyed this when I was a child but as I grew up I knew how troublesome it is when someone constantly watches your every move. Here I was free. And this was the definition of freedom for me.

A week passed…

I got adapted to this life very well but my so called princess syndrome shattered here in hostel. I learned to do all my work by myself. From laundry to waiting in a long queue in front of the hostel bathroom I was well versed with each and everything here and then after getting adapted in my hostel I also started missing my family but I was still fine thinking about my new friends that I made in the college. Most of them were my hostel mates as well and we developed a habit of sneaking into each other's room at night and sharing a chit-chat session. Truthful this was really fun compared to all the other morning activities that we perform.

"Do you guys know that the guy who works in the canteen opposite to our hostel has a girlfriend?" one of my friend whispered

"No way! I was aiming for him... huh! This is so frustrating, he is so handsome that my heart hurts thinking about him" I giggled when they were having nonsensical conversations.

"Oh did you hear that there is a mysterious man living in this area?" one of my friends spoke with seriousness on her face

'And what about that guy?' I asked her while smiling

"Don't you know? He is the rumoured psycho, who kidnaps young girls and sells their body organs... some say that he is a cannibal"

"Hey! You are joking right?" Another girl who was listening to it calmly shivered and stick close to me.

'Guys stop joking... Nilima is getting scared' still they continued to speak on the same topic just to make her tremble with fear.

"My seniors were saying that he is extremely tall, he has dark black sunken eyes, his hands are as big as our head and he smells so awful and..." before she could continue there was a knock on the door and we wondered who it might be at this late hours and at that moment Nilima hid behind me

"I don't want to die" she murmured. I laughed at her naive reply and just walked towards the door as no one had any courage left in them to open the door, I knew that it was warden for sure and she will scold us again but I was even perplexed when there was a sudden black out, I almost opened the door when everyone hugged each other and started calling me to come back and not to open the door. I knew it was warden but even I was confused so I just returned to them and sat beside everyone.

"I think I should never joke again, even I was scared because of this sudden black out" my friend whispered. The banging on the door still continued but since it was dark we sat in the same position.

'If it was warden then she would have called our names right?' It was somewhat fishy... there was no voice but banging and there was this blackout all of a sudden and because of all the horror movies that we watched together, it somehow made us anxious. After fifteen minutes the banging stopped and the lights were back again, I slept there with my friends. Since most of us were scared so we decided not to step out of the room till the next morning.

'Was it really warden? Was someone joking with us?' it was still a mystery.

The next day my friend Meera joined me in my hostel room. She was back but with an extremely shocking news...

'What? Your father abandoned you?'

"Yeah" Meera replied with a bitter smile on her face

'But... You are his daughter right? How can he abandon you like that?'

"He said that I was capable enough to earn now, he told me to not to burden him and just leave his family alone... (sobbing) he even advised me to sell my body like my mother because I deserve that!" Meera broke down. She cried endlessly as there was no one to support her. I consoled her and also came up with a solution

'Hey let's started working and earn some money for your college fees' I suggested

"Yeah... I think I should work more to earn" Meera murmured silently

'Don't worry! Even I will join you and the money we earn will be used as your fees'

"But are you sure? It will be a burden for you... you have to study and work as well and it will be a burden for you, what if you scores reduce? Then your parents will blame...."

'Come on! Cheer up! I won't tell this to my parents so we can keep it as a secret only we know'

"I am extremely thankful for all your help Sara; you just tell me anything I will do it for you"

'I was waiting for you to say that!' I grinned, looking at me Meera asked me back

"So you want to eat Omurice right? I will cook for you..."

'Hurray!' I was happy since Omurice is a Japanese dish which is my favorite food. I saw it once in a Japanese movie and craved for it, Meera was good in cooking since she did all the chores in her father's house and learned to make one and fed it to me... and since then it is my favorite food.

Meera and I started working in convenience store. We worked there as a helper and I, of course supported and helped her in that work and thus months passed, we worked and studied and thus did everything together but I found Meera acting very strange recently. She has always been normal most of the times but when she got a call from certain someone she started getting scared and also started sweating profoundly, it's like as if she is hiding something from me. I tried to ask her many times but she dismissed the topic saying that it was alright and it was her father just tormenting her.

Meera and I spent our time just like that. I always felt sorry for Meera, A girl as calm and mature as her is being tormented like this and then I realized 'how lucky I am' I have parents who support me and care for me though they tried to convince me to marry early but they just never forced me and thus for the very first time my heart-felt heavy thinking 'how I always acted willful and never considered their feelings and acted rude'

"Oh Sara, How are you dear?" My mother exclaimed when I took the initiative to call her

'Mom, I just miss you and father'

"Oh! Did something happen? Are you unwell? Don't tell me you want more pocket money again!"

'No Mom I am being serious right now! I really miss you and father' as I yelled to prove myself right my father took the phone and spoke,

"All right stop yelling and tell me how everything's going on there? Are you studying properly? Are you interested in any boy there? If so then I will reconsider your marriage proposal with my..."

'Gosh why did I even call you guys?' I smiled and hung up. But it was worth it to have them by my side to support me, they just nag all the time but I can still feel their love.

Days passed peacefully. We worked without any turbulence got our pay and as I promised I gave that money to Meera as her college fees and we still stayed together all the time. But her behavior was starting to get further more suspicious as she always hides something from me and disappeared suddenly for a day or two. I thought 'enough of these secrets now!' and finally I asked her...

"That... I met a guy and we are friends but I like him and I decided to propose him... I am still scared a bit but I am mustering up my courage"

'What?' I screamed at the top of my lungs. I was shocked.

'So all this time you were with this guy and you never told me anything about it? Am I even a friend to you?' I was extremely angry on her as she was hiding things from me

"No it isn't like that, please trust me Sara! I wanted you to be the first person to know everything about it but i was scared that you will be angry on me and just won't let me meet him again"

'So am I a villain to you now?'

"No it's not like that..."

'Then what is it like?'

"That..." she was really reluctant to share her feelings with me. I felt bad, I was her only friend and she hid it from me, it hit in a very different way. I sighed and asked,

'So where did you meet him?'

"Actually... that... I met him in a bar..." she spoke hesitantly. I was literally stunned at this point.

'What bar? What were you doing there? In that kind of place does it suit a girl like you?' I was extremely angry at this point,

'So you were in bar all this time when you suddenly went missing and stopped receiving my calls'

"I-it isn't like that at all! I was short of money; you were working so hard with me even it was affecting your studies you just didn't give up on me so how could I ask you for more? How could I be so selfish? And that's why I worked there." Before I could explode on her she continued to convince me...

"I found out that there was a vacancy for assistant cook in that bar and I worked there as a cook for two to three days a week, it was night shift and nobody took up that job and even they paid nicely. You know I cook well right? So I worked there... don't worry at all its safe for me there since I won't come in contact with customers directly" she at last convinced me by giving all these reasons and I couldn't just argue more so I agreed with her since it was her decision.

Since that day I kept on visiting that bar through it's backdoor to meet her and check on her and everything turned out to be going smoothly again. I also met Meera's crush, his name was Nisar and he was a cook in that bar. He was pretty much older from Meera but he looked like nice guy overall I guess...

Sometimes Meera skipped working in convenience store and I think I understand her pretty much now because she wanted to spend more time with Nisar and the income from bar was pretty good for her now, I even felt that she will just quit working here. I was even feeling tired working all the time without any rest and studying while working was getting hectic since I lacked enthusiasm because Meera was not here. Even I was thinking of quitting from working here. Meera was happy, Nisar was with her and we pretty much stopped communicating since Meera was always out and I was stuck in my room because of studies.

'Dating is surely good... I think I should also date someone but why nobody is interested in me? Huh! I feel like I am wasting my youth' I had all types of thoughts after that... thoughts like 'am I ugly?' 'Do I look fat?' 'My skin is so dry' 'I feel so frustrated!' started hissing in my mind. I was feeling lonely in this big city whereas my friends were dating, hanging out and enjoying their life. And while having that type of mindset he entered like a storm into my life...

III

AN ENCOUNTER WITH A HANDSOME MAN

It was a pretty usual day like any other days... I woke up and got ready for my college. Meera was in a deep sleep as she had a night shift I left the room keys with her and attended classes and after finishing my classes I went to convenience store to work and then after finishing my work I went to my hostel but there was a problem

Meera, this girl...She forget to hand over the room keys to warden and as such I just couldn't enter my room because I don't have keys with me, I couldn't wait in other's room because my other friends were still in college attending extra classes and I was waiting here. I called Meera and she luckily picked up my call,

'Hey are the room keys with you?'

"Oh! I just forgot to hand it over to warden this morning... I am sorry"

'Okay where are you I want my keys now'

"I am in bar, you can come and collect it from me" she said it casually and hung up. It was already evening and I had to go all the way to that bar which was an hour distant from my hostel, I had no other option. As I reached the bar it was almost sunset, I was running late and while I was walking with hurried steps carrying my bag, my library books I collided with someone... My books and bag fell from my hands and I fell on the floor, the person who collided with me stood still unaffected as if I was just a small mosquito in front of him. Sun was bright red and he was standing still staring at me intensely. I saw him, he was very, extremely tall man his back was facing the sun and thus I couldn't see his face clearly, it took some time for me to process what was happening with me.

He moved his hand towards me as if he was gesturing me to hold his hands. I just stared blankly at him and didn't get any hints but then I realized I was still sitting in the middle of the road with my books and bag scattered like an idiot and was staring in daze towards the man with whom I just collided. I immediately felt ashamed. I moved my hands towards him to hold his hand which was extended for me. When we clasped our hands I felt his skin, it was very soft and warm, I felt comfortable holding it and he helped me to get up. When I stood beside him I could overall feel how manly he was, he was very tall around 185 cm, wide shoulders, normal skin tone, clean shaved, well built but had a suppressive aura which makes me feel like a small and delicate rabbit around him whereas he looked like he was a predator who would swallow me if I made any mistake.

I was still staring at him blankly but he wasn't reluctant at all, he kept my small hand in his and didn't let it go.

"Sara!"

I came to my senses when I heard someone calling my name loudly, I immediately took my hand back from his but he held it strongly. I looked at him and he was grinning, I felt chills suddenly and then Meera came to me. He let go of my hands when he saw Meera glaring at him, he kneeled in front of me and picked my books and bag and handed it over to me. Sun was already set and street lights glowed. Then I clearly saw his face, he was smiling warmly, his eyes were charming and lips... why does it look so beautiful when he smiled? As I was in daze Meera shook me and I was back to my senses.

"Sara I waited for you but what are you doing here?"

'I... I was coming to you but I dashed with him and fell down' I pointed my finger towards him as if I was blaming him

"Sara right? I think your name was Sara..." he murmured my name and I shivered suddenly. His voice was very deep and husky... I was not myself. I was always a chatter box but in front of him I was speechless, I was admiring him and as well as shivering in front of him which wasn't like my usual self. Meera tried to take my books from his hands but he moved those in front of me and gestured me to take it. I calmly took my books from his hand, his skin brushed with mine. He smiled again and Meera just grabbed my arm with force and took me inside the bar through the backdoor, when he saw Meera grabbing my arm his expression were indescribable it suddenly gave me chills when he looked at me with those eyes, at that moment I realized,

'I am not myself in front of him. I always act high and mighty in front of others but in front of him I was extremely vulnerable'

Meera called me all of sudden "Sara!"

'Huh? What did you say Meera? I am sorry I wasn't actually listening to you'

"What were you doing with him?"

'Do you know him?'

"Know? I just don't even want to remember meeting that kind of guy ever again in my life"

'Why?'

"He is a man who always visits our bar and he is just kind of creepy, I am telling you he is not normal at all! But why were you holding his hand? Are you out of your mind?"

'I wasn't holding his hands, it's just that we collided and I fell down, he just extended his hand to help me get up, that's why I was holding his hand. There's nothing more to that'

"But Sara I seriously recommend you to not meet that guy ever again..."

'At least tell me why you are warning me so seriously?'

"He... is a customer in our bar and he keeps smiling, at first I thought he was very handsome and a kind customer but then Nisar told me that he lost his family when he was very young and he stays all alone, and..." she was hesitant to speak further then I urged her to continue

"He is a psycho!" Meera screamed with her eyes closed

'You are lying aren't you? Meera'

"Huh? N-no I am not, whatever I said was true"

'I know just by looking at you that you are lying, so tell me why are you lying about the man you don't even know?'

Meera smiled awkwardly and handed over the keys to me, she just rushed towards the kitchen to avoid answering my questions. At this point of time I was sure that something was wrong with her,

'I should avoid staying with her as much as possible' was my conclusion

At this point everything was becoming a mystery to me. Meera, my childhood friend was acting strange; the guy I met was smiling and kept grinning. He was even murmuring my name...

"Sara right? I think your name was Sara..." I recalled his husky deep voice and my cheeks were already burning hot, I was blushing but then I thought he really was my type, I always wanted to marry a guy who was like him.

I just fell asleep as soon as I placed my head on the pillow. Next day I woke up and went to college as usual and then I went to convenience store to work. Today was my last day working in this store; I just stared at my surrounding to have a glance for the last time before my duty was over. I heard a sound of the door opening when I looked towards the door I found him.

The same guy from yesterday, who collided with me and who was smiling harmlessly was standing in front of me near the counter.

"Where can I find cigarettes?" he asked me with a deep husky voice. He was not even looking at me and was just behaving as if he doesn't know me at all.

"Excuse me..."

'Sir we don't sell cigarettes here.'

"Oh I see... then where can I find it?"

'Sorry sir I have no idea about that'

"I see" he just left without even looking at me.

'Did he just forget what happened yesterday?' I wondered. I was simply worrying having all the imaginations but for him it was just a normal encounter that he forgot. Well I think I should just forget them as well.

'But that guy was surely very handsome' I grinned thinking about him and just like that my duty was over. I hugged the shop owner; she was a very kind lady who supported me and my friend.

I concentrated in my studied after that day, since exams were near I wanted to score good and just like that a year passed. I was very well versed in this city now, Meera and Nisar are together for almost an year and they really are a happy couple. I was still single, nerd and jerk as always. I never met that handsome man with whom I dashed near the bar again. Thinking about that I guess it was just a coincidence and nothing more than that.

IV
KIDNAPPED AND IMPRISONED

"Baby get up... I bought breakfast for you... come on sweet heart wake up..." this deep husky voice I heard it somewhere, where was it again? Why is it dark everywhere? Where am I? Help! I want to get out of here! Help! I was screaming but my voice wasn't coming out. What is happening with me? Help!

".....ra"

'Who is this?'

"Sara... wake up..."

I woke up abruptly and breathed heavily

"Sara are you okay? You were sweating and breathing so hard while you were asleep"

'Maybe it was a nightmare' I sighed, it was just a dream. Maybe I dreamt about it because I watched a horror movie yesterday, gosh! I was frustrated today without any reason. When I woke up from bed I glanced towards my watch.

'Oh my god I am late!' I got ready and immediately rushed to college, I didn't had my breakfast because I was late, I didn't had much of an appetite these days and because of that I started skipping my dinner. My friends often told me that I lost some weight but hearing them saying this out of worry I was feeling a bit guilty. College was not that far from my hostel but I still had to walk some distance and as I was walking I suddenly felt dizzy.

'Maybe because I couldn't sleep properly I am feeling dizzy' I thought and just kept walking. There was an alley which I had to pass to reach the college, this alley was often crowd less, but today there was no one here, maybe because it was still early morning. But as I walked I felt someone was following me and then someone grabbed my hand tightly and pulled me. A white cloth was placed near my nose and as I breath in I felt like I was losing my consciousness and my body felt heavy... I knew that someone was trying to kidnap me but I had very less strength left in my body to fight against that person and soon I closed my eyes from all those blurry vision.

"....I was ...... for you..."

Someone was whispering something but I couldn't understand what was happening to me. My eyelids were heavy and I was extremely sleepy.

When I woke up I saw a beautiful ceiling, it was elegant unlike my hostel room. My eyes were still blurry but I was fully conscious. when I sat up on that bed, I found myself sleeping on the bed of a beautiful room, the room pretty much empty but it was elegantly designed, when I tried to get up from that bed I found my right hand was tied to bed with a chain even my legs were tied to that bed like I was some prisoner. There was no one in that room except for me. It was quiet and somewhat dark...

'I think it's evening now' I murmured. I tried to recall what exactly was happening. I then remembered the last fragments of my memory and realized that I was kidnapped by someone and I am being imprisoned in this bedroom, tied to the bed so as to not escape from here. I panicked and started shouting for help and maybe he heard me screaming at the top of my lungs, the bedroom door opened and he entered. I thought someone kidnapped me for trafficking or for money but when I saw him I was stupefied.

'You? What are you doing here?' I recognized him immediately. He was the same man whom I met near the bar, it was surely him because I could never forget him.

"So you still remember me?" he whispered and smiled as if he was happy that I remember him.

'Why am I being confined here? What do you want? If you want money then I will give it to you... if you are thinking of human trafficking then don't forget that my father is a policeman and he has extremely high contacts!' I tried to threaten him but he just stood near the door staring at me intensely without uttering a single word. His distorted face was smiling again.

"Ha-ha! Did you think I brought you here for money? Just look around this room... does it seem like I lack money? And if I was thinking of human trafficking then I should have imprisoned you in a very shabby place, for example basement? Ha-ha... why would I let you sleep in my room with the most luxurious bed and chains which causes least pain when you try to move around?" He was suppressing his laugh while answering my questions. He was treating me like a fool.

'Then why did you kidnap me?' I was really angry at this point, he was really annoying. His gaze on me was very cold and warm at the same time which made me feel extremely uncomfortable.

"Why did I bring you here? Isn't it simple? I brought the thing which belongs to me back"

'What?'

"You really are very naive aren't you?"

He looked like a true psycho to me and then I recalled what Meera said to me about him

"He is a man who always visits our bar and he is just creepy, I am telling you he is not normal at all! He is a psycho!"

'Just let me go!' I screamed and tried to remove those shackles. He walked closer towards me with an indescribable look on his face. He sat beside me on the same bed. His long slim fingers caressed my hair and he was patting me, I grabbed his hand as my left hand was free from chains, He smiled back brightly and held my hand in his. I tried to break free from him but he pulled me closer to him and whispered

"Finally... (Breaths) I can finally touch you now. You just don't know how long I have been holding myself. I was going crazy from just looking at you but couldn't touch you. But now I will always be by your side and will never leave you alone"

'You are crazy! So you were following me everywhere all this time and kidnapped me? Have you gone nuts? I am telling you... you still have time, I don't know you and I won't report you so just let me go because if my father gets to know that I am kidnapped then he will surely take action against you!' I warned him and glared at him angrily. I thought he will listen to me because no matter how strong you are you have some fear in you, as i was glaring at him his face which was smiling sweetly turned dark, he came close to me and suddenly grabbed my hair,

'Ah!' I screamed in pain

"I am being nice to you that doesn't mean I am a pushover... I hate it when people take me lightly and ignore my feelings. Do I look like a joke to you? I brought you here because I want to keep by my side all the time and you think I will let you go that easily?" He whispered angrily

'I said leave me! I don't want to be with you!' I screamed, but then he slapped me. His slap didn't sting much but the fact that I was slapped made me cry. I was never treated this poorly ever in my life, at least I was never really hit by my parents even thought they scolded me most of the time.

'You are a psycho!' I cried and broke away from his grip and hid my face in blanket; I was scared that this man will beat me to death if I talked anything again. I decided to just ignore his existence and wait for help. I was very confident that my father will surely come to find me and break me free from these shackles and take me home.

I was scared as well as desperate. He just sat beside me on the bed without any movements, I could hear his murmurs as he was cursing and clenching the bed sheet and after a long pause he broke the silence,

"Hey... d-don't turn away from me. I was... I just lost control and slapped you; it was never my intention to slap you like that. I don't like it when you are in pain" he slowly touched my shoulder though there was a blanket but still I could feel his long fingers touching my shoulders and I don't know why but tears started forming in my eyes again and I was crying, he heard my sobs and kept rubbing my shoulders feeling guilty for his actions

"I won't do that again... I promise so just don't think about leaving and stay by my side, if you resist much then it will be painful for you..." he wasn't consoling me but rather he was threatening me. He was telling me to shut up and quit resisting; if I didn't then he would just repeat the same actions again.

I was sure at this point that he is crazy. Nothing can restrain him; if I try to escape then he will surely harm me again so I have to act sensible hence forth. I should never talk to him and go against him. He just sat beside me for some time and rubbed my hands then he got up and walked away. When he felt I came out of the blanket and saw that he was gone. The room which was a bit bright was completely dark now. It was night and the room was cold, I was all alone in this place. There was no one beside me. I missed my parents and cried endlessly as time passed my tears were dry and I mustered up my courage with the hope that they will find me.

He entered the room after sometime,

"Why is the room so dark? Didn't you turn on the lights?" he asked. He was acting so normal as if he forgot his actions from earlier and just placed some food in front of me.

"Oh I forgot, you are tied to bed so you couldn't move and turn on the lights right? Don't worry I will always come to you and stay with you; sorry I wasn't with you just now. I went to prepare dinner for you. When you are with me you don't need to worry about anything and just rest peacefully. I was really worried when you quit eating and turned so skinny... you were so healthy and cheerful when we met but after a year you turned so skinny and gloomy... (Sigh) you know I thought that I should just keep you by my side" he was talking but I remained silent. I just listened to him and didn't reply. When he saw that I was ignoring him, he suddenly grabbed my chin

"I am talking to you Sara... don't you think you should look at me and reply to me?" When our eyes met I saw him grinning. I was scared; if I didn't reply him then he will beat me again.

'...Yes' I whispered. After hearing me he smiled widely and placed the plate in front of me. When he removed the cover and told me to have my dinner, I was stunned

'Omurice....?'

"Ah yes, it's Omurice. I heard that this is your favorite food, so I personally cooked it for you to make you happy"

He knew everything about me. He knew my favorite food which was only known to Meera and my family. He really was dangerous; I can never take him lightly and have to be on guard.

"You like my efforts right? Tell me you are happy" he gripped my wrist tightly, I was tongue-tied but I have to respond.

'Yes... thank you' I whispered. His anger seems to be disappearing and he started rubbing my wrist which was gripped tightly by him.

"Taste it Sara..." he started feeding me and I just couldn't reject him. I, very reluctantly and quietly ate all the food that he put into my mouth and swallowed it. As I finished eating, he took the plate and went away and he came back with another plate full of Omurice again.

"Taste it Sara..." he fed me again. I Just don't want to eat it. I wasn't feeling good. My stomach was upset and I was about to puke. I grabbed his hand which was feeding me

'I am full...' I looked at him and tried to force a smile.

"Really? You eat very less Sara, but I still want to feed you so open your mouth" he was very persistent, I have to divert his concentration because if this continues then I will fall sick and can't plan my escape.

I gently touched his hand and spoke

"You... what is your name?"

As i questioned him his eyes widened and he immediately pushed the plate away.

"I am Karan..." he smiled. His smile was so dazzling and beautiful that I forgot he was my kidnapper and I was his hostage. It wasn't fair! He looked so innocent and harmless that I completely forgot he was the same person who kidnapped me and slapped me.

V
PAINFUL REALITY OF CONFINEMENT

Days passed but there was no one who came to my rescue. But I still had some hope, I was tied to this bed all the time. When I felt sad and cried, he let me walk around this room but he held my hands tightly so I can't run away. He let me bath and use toilet but then as soon as I was done he tied me again. I recalled one dog which I used to raise when I was very small. I fed him, walked him and I tied him around to his dog house all the time. He ran away from our house one day and I cried a lot because I missed him and was worried for him. Since then I hated animals but now I understood why that dog ran away. It just wanted to be free from shackles and roam around happily like others and I want the same now.

'I want to be free from here and get back to my normal life again...' I spent many days in that room but I was somewhat losing hope and felt helpless. Karan was getting on my nerves. Confinement was really terrible; I tried every little thing to free myself from him but it all failed. Some of my attempts were caught and I was hit by Karan and there were some attempts which were not known to him yet. I was desperate to run away from him and he was desperate to keep me close to him. We were trying to achieve what we wanted so much that we didn't knew we were hurting each other.

I was really tired now and I was losing my mind.

'Let him beat me to death today!' I thought. '

It's better to die then to stay like this' I was ready to die and I was extremely courageous today. I decided that I will force him either in kill me or release me.

'Let me go Karan' I said sternly looking straight into his eyes

"Sara, what are you saying?"

'You know that I don't like you! Why are you forcing me to live my life like a doll?'

"Sara..."

'I am just tired of everything! I just hate everything that you are doing to me! I feel suffocated! Just release me Karan because if you don't do that then I will kill myself!' I took out the fork which I hide from him when he brought me food last time and was about to stab myself but then he gripped my hand tightly'

"I shouldn't have left your left hand untied..." he pulled me close, held my waist tightly and whispered into my ears.

"Huh! I just can't..." he tightened his grip on my waist and leaned towards me with his head on my shoulders. My right hand and legs were tied, I was sitting on the bed and he was holding my left hand tightly while leaning on me... I should push him away but... I felt my shoulder was getting wet. It was him! He was crying. He cried for a very long time and then he released his grip around me. For the very first time I saw his vulnerable side, his eyes were swollen and his ears were red, he breathed heavily and his body temperature rose. He looked like a wounded beast which can attack anytime to protect himself from the harm.

He suddenly hovered on me and I was underneath him within a second, before I could process what was happening to me he removed the blanket which was covering me and I could feel that the chains were removed from my hands and legs as well. His movement were so quick that I was confused what he was doing with me.

"I... can't control myself any more; these emotions which are rising in me are very new that I just can't understand them. Tell me if it hurts." Was what he whispered.

'What do you...' before I could continue he devoured my lips and sucked them. He was kissing me so gently but roughly at the same time that I felt my body was getting numb. He placed my hands on his shoulders and caressed my body. From lips to cheek, cheek to neck, he just kept planting small kisses and sucking me. This feeling was something which was very new to me as well.

'I should separate him from me but I... I was instead pulling him close to my body'

'I was hugging him very close to me as if he was my lifeline. My body was turning hot wherever he kissed and my brain stopped working. I started liking his touches on my body and moaned when I couldn't endure it.

Everything was new to me. It was painful at first but then the pain replaced with pleasure and I was feeling guilty but my body was asking for some more. His touches, his kisses and his caress everything was so good that I was asking him for more. I just don't know what was wrong with me. I and Karan were so much immersed in each other that our deed continued till dawn. I was tired and just fainted, I just had no energy to raise my body and cover it with blanket, but Karan did that for me. He covered his and my body and hugged me tightly in his arms as if we were one. He was patting me and his action was so gentle that it was hard to believe that the beast earlier was him.

I knew I will be embarrassed tomorrow, I knew I was extremely shameless but I just can't control my desire. My desire took over my rationality. And I started considering my situation as normal, I was slowly turning insane. I slept in his arms peacefully after thinking all these worries would disappear if he was beside me.

VI
HIS LIFE, HIS LONELINESS, HIS DESPERATION

Bright and warm sun rays kept disturbing me from sleeping, I turned around to avoid those rays and he covered me up as if to hide me from those rays and protect my precious sleep. One hand was around my waist and I used his other hand as my pillow. I slept some more and after sometime I woke up when something kept poking my cheeks disturbing me from sleeping.

"Aren't you acting like a kitten? Cuddly, cute and innocent, acting all pure in front of me and sleeping peacefully in my arms..."

'Um... I am not a kitten' I murmured.

"if you are not a kitten then what are you?"

'Um...'

"Hey... it's time for your breakfast wake up"

'Um... I don't want to' I grumbled and snuggled

'Wait... something's wrong' I felt something weird, when I opened my eyes with difficulty I saw him

'Ah! What are you doing? What? Oh Gosh! Y-you did that to me right? I hate you!' I started throwing pillows on him and he blocked them, then he suddenly pulled my arm and whispered in my ears.

"You hate me that much?"

As he questioned me I was just motionless. Do I really hate him? I got a very prompt answer from my heart... No I just don't hate him because if I hated him then I wouldn't sleep so shamelessly with him yesterday, if I hated him I should have hated his touch but I am really liking it. I felt that even if he slaps me now... I will accept it gladly because I may be wrong somewhere. Maybe he was trying to protect me and I am causing trouble for him. Gosh! What am I thinking? I was turning insane! I... I like it when he mutilates my body what kind of rubbish thinking is this?

'I don't know anything about you except for your name, how can I like a person about whom I know nothing?'

"Is it so? Then if I tell you about me then will you stay by my side forever and never leave me?" when he asked me this question all of sudden I was scared to answer him. If I said I will stay by his side forever then he will tell me about him which I was dying to know but if I said I will not then he won't tell me anything. I was scared to promise but I still wanted to know...

"So you don't want to be with me right?" he said, his eyes turned cold and I replied

'Yes! I will stay by your side forever so please tell me!' I ended up falling in his trap. Have you heard? 'Curiosity killed the cat' I was that cat in this situation.

"Okay, so you know... this bedroom in which you are in is my mine. I spent most of my time in this house. This house means everything to me and as such I bought you here. I... to be exact I pretty much hated my father. My father was very rich and he spent his time away from my mother in other women's arms, since theirs was an arranged marriage he was forced to marry my mother and gave birth to me but he never really loved my mother and me. But contrary to his feeling my mother loved him dearly and she tried to get his attention in every possible way but he hated her. My mother slowly was turning mentally ill and she started having seizers... she often hated me and abused me. She used to burn me or cut me sometimes, she even tried to kill me saying that I looked like my father and she hates him, she was my mother but her abuses were so extreme that I started hating everyone. I always locked myself in this room and cried. Soon the wounds caused by my mother started getting visible and was finally noticed by my father. He stopped her and sent her to the asylum, when he felt sorry for me and came to console me, it was already very late." I silently listened to him; the expression on his face was very pathetic I wanted to hug him because he looks very lonely.

"I hated when someone touched me... it felt like something was going to swallow me and I started confining myself into this house. My father was helpless and sent me to a psychiatrist but I was still scared, I especially hated when any women touched me, maybe because of that my father was getting worried. He passed away feeling guilty for the wounds he caused on me due his ignorance and I was left all alone, I handed over my father's business to my cousin, he works and takes care of everything. He is a good person." He had a bitter smile on his face which made me feel uncomfortable

"Then... when I visited the bar that day I met you." He looked at me and smiled sweetly. His smile took away all my anxiety

"You were the first person I touched comfortably, when we collided I just forgot all kind of discomfort, to check whether that is true I touched your hand and it truly was a miracle for me. I tried my best to keep you by my side till now, but if you think I am selfish again... then... you can just leave..." Before he could say anything I just hugged him very tightly in my arms. I recalled the burn marks and scars that was on his body yesterday, it looked extremely painful to me. He was just a small, naive child. He didn't deserve that hatred.

'Those scars which I saw yesterday was it your mother who did that?'

He just nodded and said nothing. I felt very sad, my heart was breaking and with those emotions I just said,

'I will never leave you alone. I will always be with you as I promised earlier' when heard those words I felt that he was trembling... he was just a wounded child who was looking for warmth when he felt cold and I think he finally found his warmth in my arms.

'Curiosity killed the cat, but satisfaction brought it back' and I was satisfied with my decision now.

VII

I LOVE YOU...

The days I spent with him were the very peaceful ones in my life. I felt like I was on the seventh cloud, he treated me very well and very preciously. Though my nights were really hectic, he was really a beast who was out of control most of the time and as a result my body was completely filled with his bite marks. My waist was very sore when I woke every morning but I also took all my revenge on him. I made him cook and work tirelessly but he was still absolutely fine. The chains around my hands and legs were removed most of the time but still I was confined in those as if he was really anxious.

One day, Karan was massaging my waist to relieve my pain and I was enjoying it when I suddenly heard sound of utensils, I immediately sat up and asked

'Who is it? I heard some noise down there Karan'

"Oh that? It must be servants. Ignore them baby and have a good rest"

'Did you just say servants? Huh? But you told me that all the work in this house was done by you!'

"Oh did I say that? I must have forgotten about it"

'What? You forgot to tell me such an important thing? So that's how it is! I was really wondering how you had so much energy despite working so much in home but now I got it! You were just idling around and tortured me at night and I was satisfied thinking that you were really working hard and I was getting my revenge on you!' I blurted all my frustration out but then I realised... 'Oh shit!' I immediately covered my mouth

"So you wanted revenge on me?" his smile was truly a sinister one.

'N-no it's not like that let me explain'

"Come here... let me show what revenge is...."

'Gosh he truly is a beast who keeps swallowing me raw'

When I woke up, my body was really sore but he was staring at me looking all satisfied and happy.

'My waist hurts massage it for me' I whined.

"Oh really, But I have decided not to massage it hence forth, that's my revenge" he smiled innocently.

'Please I am sorry... please I love you right sweetheart?'

"What?"

'Um... What?'

"Say that again!"

'I am sorry?'

"The words next to that"

'I love you.... sweet. Heart'

"Huh!" he sighed when I called him cutely.

"I will massage after some more rounds"

'What?'

And I learned a special lesson after that "Never ever act cute and sweet after spending a night with your man because you can make it awake again"

VIII
A SEARCH FOR MISSING SARA

"What Sara is missing?" Sara's father was shocked and was unable to digest these words.

"Sorry uncle I just don't know where she is and I tried to find her everywhere but she just disappeared when she left this morning and she didn't come home yet." Meera was much panicked because Sara was found nowhere; She feared that they may blame her for Sara's disappearance.

"I am coming tomorrow with my wife, book a room for us to stay there" Sara's father ordered Meera and hung up.

"Nisar I think Sara is in a big trouble now, she is surely kidnapped"

"Don't worry Meera... it's not your fault that she disappeared." Nisar tried to console Meera but Meera was extremely worried for Sara. She felt that it was her fault that Sara disappeared and she could just do nothing.

The very next day Sara's father visited their hostel and got some clues. According to Meera Sara left to attend classes but she disappeared. Sara's father called his friend and asked for some help. A search team of Sara's father and his friends who all were on duty officer searched for each and every clue. According to them Sara entered an alley but she didn't come out of it, there was no CCTV'S in that alley and it was difficult to know who kidnapped her. As Sara entered in that alley the CCTV recorded her but the strangest thing was there was no one who entered that alley half an hour ago before Sara entered and nobody left after Sara entered. The case was very confusing to solve and clues were very least. Sara's father felt helpless as he couldn't do anything to find his daughter but he was desperate.

He didn't get dejected and finally took Ajay's help. Ajay was the same person with whom he wanted to marry his daughter. Ajay was ready to help him find his daughter. A search was conducted and finally they reached to a meaningful conclusion...

"She wasn't kidnapped but willingly escaped with him" Ajay concluded.

"It is not possible Ajay! I know my daughter. She was not in that kind of relationship with any man." Sara's father tried to convince Ajay.

"But there is not even a slight hint of her being kidnapped! If she was kidnapped then they at least would have called us to state their demands for releasing her, I have even searched and caught most of the trafficking cases in this city but she was found nowhere. So what can I conclude at the end? It is clear that she willingly ran away with her boyfriend and they planned it as kidnapping."

"But Sara would never do that, she was never in that kind of relationship with any man" Sara's father tried to justify it.

"This is kidnapping." Ajay's father who was listening to his son and Sara's father's argument smiled calmly.

"Father, I don't think this is kidnapping!" Ajay was a bit upset when his father stated his judgement to be wrong. It hurt his pride as he worked tirelessly for weeks to find Sara.

"I think the kidnapper is very clever. He, not only kidnap her, he also left no clue for us which made us believe that Sara willingly went with him."

"How can you be so sure father?"

"Did you see the alley carefully? There are several houses here and I think he took their help. And the fact that Sara will pass from that alley exactly at that time was known to him. It means there is someone who is informing about our each and every move to him. I mean…" Ajay's father glanced at Sara's father and he got his hint.

*Slap "where is Sara?"

"Uncle, I really don't know anything about her whereabouts…" *slap

Sara's father slapped Meera twice but she still didn't spill the truth, at last they were left with no option and they took her to police station to get her confession. Meera was often beaten to death by her father and she really didn't feel anything. Getting confession from her was quite difficult. At some point Sara's father pitied Meera. He was feeling guilty that maybe his decision was wrong and it was his biasness towards Meera that he felt she was involved in it. Ajay was frustrated as there was no confession from her and Ajay's father after days said something unexpected.

"Bring Nisar here" when he announced that in front of Meera, her emotionless self flinched greatly.

"I think Nisar should also be investigated the way Miss Meera was investigated right?" at his words Meera immediately started pleading

"No! Don't do anything to him! I will tell you everything! Nisar is innocent and he has nothing to do about Sara's disappearance"

Sara's father was shocked, all this time he thought that he wronged Meera but that was not it.

Meera truly loved Nisar and he was like a precious family to her. Meera was never loved by her family and Nisar gave her that Love which she longed for.

Meera finally broke her silence and explained her meeting with Karan.

The day Sara met Karan for the very first time, Meera was there with her. Meera always was jealous and had a king of inferiority complex against Sara. "Sara has everything, loving family, beauty, intelligence, money but why not her?" she always questioned. When she and Sara came to the city for the first time, she decided that she will shine this time for sure but....

"Your friend is really beautiful Meera..." Nisar said this to Meera when he met Sara. Meera was extremely worried that she will surely steal Nisar as well from her and thus she started badmouthing about Sara to Nisar so that he could have a bad impression about her, Nisar was her crush and she wanted to keep him close to her as she loved him and after some time everything was going well. Nisar proposed to her, he ignored Sara and she was the happiest woman as she got all she wanted but then one day her father visited her and asked for some money from her when she rejected and declared that she no longer wants to see him, her father went away. Her step mother and sister left her father because of his debts and gambling. But then one day some unknown men who looked very dangerous chased her and asked her to pay her father's debt. When she complained to police, those men threatened her by beating Nisar and when she was in such a deep plight, Karan appeared before her.

"I know he was planning to kidnap her, but he pays me so well that I was free from that debt and even purchased our own house. All I told him was about Sara, he wanted to know everything about her and I just told him. I don't know anything after that"

"Do you have his address or number?"

"I... have his number" and then Meera was released but only for a short period to spend some time with Nisar. Sara's father filed a complaint against her for helping Karan in his daughter's kidnapping.

IX

FREE FROM CONFINEMENT

Karan and I were having a good time. I was free from all the worries only thinking about Karan. One day Karan was stroking my stomach.

'What's wrong?' I asked him

"I was just wondering why you didn't get pregnant still. I mean we did it so much, at this rate I should have heard some good news from you."

'Why do you want me to be pregnant so early? I am still young for that.'

"Come on. Twenty three is not that young, I was thinking that if you gave birth to my baby you will never leave my side and will be always with me" he said and started snuggling in my arms.

'No. I don't want to bear the child yet!' I tried to tease him.

"Really? Then I am left with no other option" he started smirking and it was very rough that day. Maybe he was angry, so he was really aggressive.

Then that specific evening I woke up from some loud noises... I really couldn't sleep properly, when I tried to open my eyes, I saw Karan struggling and some men were trying to suppress him. I could also hear my father's voice calling my name... 'This may be some kind of irritating dream again' I thought but fatigue over took me and I fell asleep again. Karan and I did it almost every day and because of that it was too much for my body to handle it. So I just couldn't blame myself for not waking up.

*****

Sara wasn't dreaming instead it was reality. Ajay and his father enquired the alley once again and this time they found the main clue to solve the case. According to a house owner who was living in that alley stated that there was a strange man who rented a room in his house and stayed there for only two months. He lived all alone and looked like he wasn't lacking any money and then the disappearance of Sara was clear.

Karan stayed in that house and kept an eye on Sara, after sometime he kidnapped her and kept her in that room for two days, at that time Sara's father just came to city to find about his daughter. He kept on injecting medicines in her so she won't gain consciousness and start screaming, then he took her to his house and planned the timing completely. When Sara woke up in the evening she believed that she was kidnapped that morning. Overall he was very clever. He left no clues except Meera. He believed that Meera was tight-lipped and nobody will have suspicion on her, but his plan failed when Meera disclosed everything. Through the bank transactions in the Meera's account, they found Karan's address and they even caught him.

Karan was sleeping peacefully beside Sara and was off-guard and thus they arrested him. Sara's father found Sara unconscious although she was sleeping but in his eyes his daughter was kidnapped and molested. His daughter was covered in a thin blanket and there were some bruises on her neck. Sara's father consumed with anger started beating Karan and then they arrested Karan and took Sara home.

*****

When I woke up, I found myself dressed and then found out that I was in my room, it was my bedroom and not Karan's. I woke up immediately and sprinted towards the main door, there I found my mom, whose eyes were swollen and asked

'Mom... why was I here? I was in his house right? Where is he?' she looked at me and started crying again. She thought I was turning crazy because of all those abuses. She told me to sleep and called a nurse and they injected some stabilizers in me.

I then woke up the next day and found that it was very dark in my room,

'I guess it's night now' I immediately rushed to escape from my house and to meet Karan. Strange isn't it? I was crying to go home and see my parents and even tried to kill myself just to go back home when I was kidnapped and now... when I am finally back to my house with my parents I don't feel any happiness and want Karan back. I was crazy in other's eyes but for me... I love Karan. As I rushed towards the stairs, I suddenly slipped and fell down. It hit my head and I passed out but my stomach was also aching very badly.

When I woke up again I found myself in the hospital and my mother was crying very loudly and hugged me...

"My daughter.... how can these things happen to my daughter.... you are only twenty three years old and was

abused and even pregnant and now you lost that child…
it might have been so painful for you. It was all my fault,
I should have listened to your father and should have
married you off"

After hearing her words I lost my mind. 'I was pregnant
with Karan's child?'

X

SOMEONE'S DEATH LEAD TO OTHER'S FREEDOM

I spent my time in hospital for almost two months not to treat my physical condition but to treat my mental illness as I told my parents what happened between me and Karan and I even informed them that I loved Karan and I wanted to keep this child but they said,

"I think you have gone crazy! You should treat yourself" and thus they just kept sending me to a psychiatrist and tried to treat me.

"It wasn't love Sara, you were manipulated by him" the psychiatrist kept repeating same things again and again so as to erase Karan from my memory completely and they were succeeding. I was really tender at that time, I went through so much that my mind wasn't stable. But still I decided to meet Karan and ask him personally that, was his love true for me? Will he take me away from this hell and let me stay with him? I called Meera but she didn't respond. I knew Meera was the only outsider who can help me but I couldn't contact her and then after two months when I came back home, Nisar visits me.

"Do you know him Sara?" my father asked me.

'Yes father' I replied. Nisar looked harmless and after enquiring him for long time father let him meet me. Nisar lied to my father and said that he was my friend, he hid the truth about his relationship with Meera, and at that point I knew he has come for something else. When I took him out to our balcony to have a talk his eyes were filled with tears,

"Meera was arrested..."

'What, But why?'

"She was involved in your kidnapping and she helped Karan by passing all the information so she was arrested for helping a criminal and..." he stopped and took a letter out of his pocket.

"This... this is Karan's last words for you"

'Last... last words?' my eyes were filled with tears and i grabbed Nisar's collar

'What happened to him? Tell me how you found this letter!'

"It's been a week, he died a week ago. Maybe he knew he was going to die so he met Meera and asked her to pass on this letter to you. Meera handed over this responsibility to me and here... take this and treasure it"

The emotions which I felt was indescribable, I asked him only one thing...

'How did he die? What happened to him?' Nisar looked hesitant but then he said,

"Meera told me this when she met me last time. Karan met her once, gave this letter and told her about his decision, I can just tell you vaguely about what happened, is that okay with you?"

'Yes' I replied and held that letter with caution in my hands.

*****

Karan was arrested. Sara's parents took her and he was imprisoned. Ajay was totally frustrated as he couldn't rest for days because of this piece of trash named Karan. And he took out all his anger on him and beat him to death. Karan was bleeding, starving but he still held onto his life very dearly because if he was alive and survived he could meet Sara again. But then one day Ajay's father came to meet him.

"How are you young man?"

"None of your business"

Ajay's father grabbed Karan's face and he felt disgusted as he was touched by him. His illness was triggering him again.

"I pity Sara... she was such an adorable child. I was very happy when I saw her; she was a lovely daughter for me. I even decided to make her my daughter-in-law but then a small pest like you destroyed her life completely."

"Sir, I love Sara"

"Love? WHAT KIND OF RUBBISH IS THIS?" He was angry and screamed.

"You know how badly Sara is suffering because of you? She was pregnant with your child and even lost it! At such a young age she suffered so much just because of you and you call this love?"

"Sara... is... she okay? I didn't know she was pregnant! Let me go! I want to see her"

"You know why Sara is suffering such a big misfortune in her life?"

"Please I want to meet Sara"

"If you didn't exist in her life then she would have completed her studies, married my son and lived happily with a respectful life but you... because of you she lost everything! Do you still deserve to see Sara after causing so much harm to her?"

Ajay's father kept blaming and manipulating Karan every day. Karan couldn't meet Sara and Ajay's father kept blaming him for all the misfortune Sara suffered.

"Dad, why do you keep visiting him?" Ajay asked his father.

"I want him to take the initiative of finishing his life and we have to do this before Sara comes back to her sense and tries to search him. He is a very wealthy person and his cousin can do anything to bail him out, I want to punish him for all his crimes but I don't think he will be getting the punishment he deserves. And besides Sara should confess against him and that seems impossible as Sara is turning crazy for him. So the only way to punish him is torturing him mentally and triggering him so much that..."

"...That he finally kills himself." Ajay continued

"The people like him should be punished properly so that they won't be alive to commit such crime again; he destroyed Sara's life, her happiness completely. Do you think she will be happy living with that psychopath? If not for him her life would have been so beautiful" Ajay's father exclaimed. He met Sara when she was very young and often played with her. Though she was the daughter of his subordinate, he treated her like his own daughter but then he was transferred and couldn't meet her again. When he met Sara's father after a long time in a park, the first thing he asked him was about Sara. Though Sara's father invited him to his house he just kept insisting that he will meet her some other day. In fact he planned Sara's marriage with his son but then he met Sara in the most pathetic state.

The girl whom he wanted to see happy and treated like his own child was in such a state. He didn't feel any remorse for his actions against Karan because he believed that if Karan disappears only then Sara can move on in her life.

*****

Karan wrote a letter for Sara and asked to meet Meera. He begged Ajay's father to let him do this and they allowed him. Karan explained everything to Meera and asked her to hand over that letter to Sara.

"I will do this favour on you but I want to ask you something. If your answer is satisfying then I will do as you say"

"What is it?" Karan replied

"Did you really love Sara or was it just an obsession and manipulation as others said?" Meera asked.

Karan smiled "It was obsession at first but now I want to see her happy and live her life to the fullest. I desperately want her to forget me and move on in her life and be happy so that's why I am taking this decision, isn't it love?"

Meera smiled and took that letter from him.

"Please give this letter to her as i don't want to worry her" Karan said.

"Yes... Goodbye partner"

Karan smiled happily... "Yes goodbye to you too..."

I Miss You, I Will Always Love You

"Now that I lost you forever... I miss you. Though I can't see your smile again, I will always engrave it into my heart. You were very dear to me, I hated you but I fell in love with you. I loved your vulnerable side that you showed only to me. I loved your sobs when we were on my bed and you were below me, your touch, your kisses, your anger, and your tantrums I love and accept everything and anything as long as it belongs to you but I just can't take it when you are taken away from me. The moment we met I lost my heart completely for you, the moment your hand touched mine I lost my sanity completely. How can I feel you again, how can I touch you again, how can I meet you again, when can I see you again was all I thought... I spent months trying to know every single thing about you, I revised each and everything about you. I was lacking in expressing my love but I was never faking my love for you. You may think it was a nightmare for you and you may forget after waking up the very next day, surrounded by your family, friends and all the other happy moments but for me... my life was revolving around you. The moments we spent together were a dream for me, a happy dream from which I never want to wake up again. The time that I spent with you is engraved and will be remembered till I take my last breath. You won't be with me when I am taking my last breath but I assure you that I will be always waiting for you. If not this life then I hope to surely meet you in my next life... my feelings for you never changed and it will never will, but I want you to be happy and see you with that beautiful smile again.

Don't cry when you won't find me after waking up because you know how sad I feel when you cry. I know this letter will reach to you a little late and I will be gone till then but my love please bear with it. When the wind blows I will caress you with my warmth.

My Love I will miss you and I will always love you...."

'These were his last words for me... he expects me to live happily after leaving me all alone and lonely, he just dig a hole in my heart which can never be filled and cured again. But he was my first and only love in this lifetime of mine. Sweetheart rest in peace, I will miss you too and I will always love you....'

THE END
STOCKHOLM SYNDROME
'Can we call it love?'

9 798885 305532